DATE DUE

			PRINTED IN U.S.A.

MEDIALOG INC
ALEXANDRIA KY 41001

A Note to Parents

Welcome to REAL KIDS READERS, a series of phonics-based books for children who are beginning to read. In the classroom, educators use phonics to teach children how to sound out unfamiliar words, providing a firm foundation for reading skills. At home, you can use REAL KIDS READERS to reinforce and build on that foundation, because the books follow the same basic phonic guidelines that children learn in school.

Of course the best way to help your child become a good reader is to make the experience fun—and REAL KIDS READERS do that, too. With their realistic story lines and lively characters, the books engage children's imaginations. With their clean design and sparkling photographs, they provide picture clues that help new readers decipher the text. The combination is sure to entertain young children and make them truly want to read.

REAL KIDS READERS have been developed at three distinct levels to make it easy for children to read at their own pace.

- LEVEL 1 is for children who are just beginning to read.
- LEVEL 2 is for children who can read with help.
- LEVEL 3 is for children who can read on their own.

A controlled vocabulary provides the framework at each level. Repetition, rhyme, and humor help increase word skills. Because children can understand the words and follow the stories, they quickly develop confidence. They go back to each book again and again, increasing their proficiency and sense of accomplishment, until they're ready to move on to the next level. The result is a rich and rewarding experience that will help them develop a lifelong love of reading.

For my husband, Tom, who created the tin can
man, and for my daughter, Julianna, who pulled
him in Maplewood's Fourth of July parade
—M. L.

Special thanks to Lands' End, Dodgeville, WI, and to
Cricket Hosiery for providing clothing.

Produced by DWAI / Seventeenth Street Productions, Inc.
Reading Specialist: Virginia Grant Clammer

Library of Congress Cataloging-in-Publication Data
Leonard, Marcia.
    The tin can man / Marcia Leonard ; photographs by Dorothy Handelman.
        p.   cm. — (Real kids readers. Level 1)
    Summary: A girl and her father build a figure out of tin cans that wins a blue ribbon.
    ISBN 0-7613-2012-1 (lib. bdg.). — ISBN 0-7613-2037-7 (pbk.)
    [1. Tin cans—Fiction. 2. Parades—Fiction. 3. Fathers and daughters—Fiction.
4. Stories in rhyme.] I. Handelman, Dorothy, ill. II. Title. III. Series.
PZ8.3.L54925Ti 1998
[E]—dc21   98-10042
                                                                              CIP
                                                                              AC

                        pbk: 10 9 8 7 6 5 4 3 2 1
                        lib: 10 9 8 7 6 5 4 3 2 1

The Tin Can Man

By Marcia Leonard

Photographs by Dorothy Handelman

The Millbrook Press

Brookfield, Connecticut

Nan had a plan
and one tin can.

She had one can.
Then she had two,

then one that was old,
and one that was new.

She and her dad
went door to door.

10

They got more cans . . .
and more and more.

They made two arms.

They made two legs.

They made a man
of wood and pegs.

The cans went on
to make his skin.

They made two eyes.
They made him grin.

23

Nan and the man
are set to go.

25

She can pull him
to and fro.

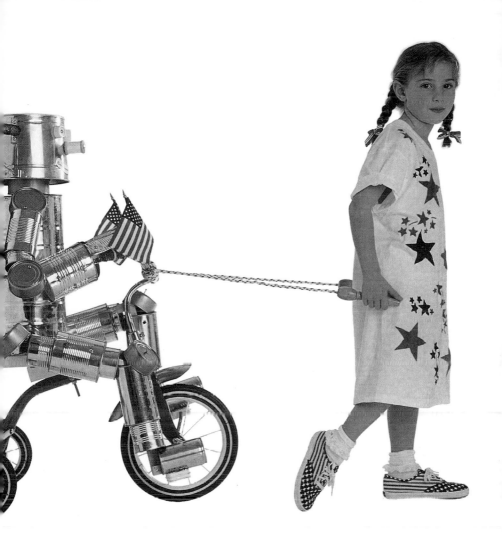

They go with Dad
and all the rest.

29

The tin can man—
and Nan—are best!

Reading with Your Child

1. Try to read with your child at least twenty minutes each day, as part of your regular routine.
2. Keep your child's books in one convenient, cozy reading spot.
3. Read and familiarize yourself with the Phonic Guidelines below.
4. Ask your child to read *The Tin Can Man* out loud. If he or she has difficulty with a word:
   - Help him or her decode the word phonetically. (Say, "Try to sound it out.")
   - Encourage him or her to use picture clues. (Say, "What does the picture show?")
   - Ask him or her to use context clues. (Say, "What would make sense?")
5. If your child still doesn't "get" the word, tell him or her what it is. Don't wait for frustration to build.
6. Praise your beginning reader. With your enthusiasm and encouragement, your child w' go from one success to the next.

Phonic Guidelines

Use the following guidelines to help your child read the words in *The Tin Can Man*.

Short Vowels
When two consonants surround a vowel, the sound of the vowel is usually short. This means you pronounce *a* as in apple, *e* as in egg, *i* as in igloo, *o* as in octopus, and *u* as in umbrella. Short-vowel words in this story include: *can, dad, got, had, him, his, legs, man Nan, pegs, set.*

Short-Vowel Words with Beginning Consonant Blends
When two different consonants begin a word, they usually blend to make a combined sound. Words in this story with beginning consonant blends include: *plan, skin.*

Short-Vowel Words with Ending Consonant Blends
When two different consonants end a word, they usually blend to make a combined sour Words in this story with ending consonant blends include: *best, rest.*

R-Controlled Vowels
When a vowel is followed by the letter *r*, its sound is changed by the *r*. Words in this stor with r-controlled vowels include: *arms, her.*

Double Consonants
When two identical consonants appear side by side, one of them is silent. Double-consonant words in this story include: *pull.*

Sight Words
Sight words are those words that a reader must learn to recognize immediately—by sight-instead of by sounding them out. They occur with high frequency in easy texts. Sight words not included in the above categories are: *a, all, and, are, go, made, make, new, old on, one, she, that, the, then, they, to, two, was, went, with.*